Wolf Cry

Jutta Goetze

sundance
A Haights Cross Communications Company

a black dog book

Published by Sundance Publishing
P.O. Box 1326, 234 Taylor Street, Littleton, MA 01460

Copyright © text Jutta Goetze

First published 1999 as Phenomena by
Horwitz Martin
A Division of Horwitz Publications Pty Ltd
55 Chandos St., St. Leonards NSW 2065 Australia

Exclusive United States Distribution: Sundance Publishing

ISBN 0-7608-4946-3

Printed in Canada

Contents

Author's Note 5

Chapter 1 **Min and Jim** 7

Chapter 2 **Grandfather Russ** 20

Chapter 3 **Ruff** 31

Chapter 4 **Running with the Pack** 49

Chapter 5 **Caught** 59

Chapter 6 **Coming Back from the Wild** 75

Animal Facts 92

Where to from Here? 95

Dedication

In the cemetery in Midnapore, India, there are the unmarked graves of two girls, Amala and Kamala, the wolf-children.

I dedicate this book to them. The graves of children should never be forgotten.

Author's Note

I've never been to India. So I did a great deal of research when I wrote this book. Of course, having traveled to India in the books I've read, I now want to visit in person. I am fascinated by its people, animals, landscape, and stories. For me, writing this book has opened doors.

And I learned a great deal about wolves. I hadn't realized how big a part wolves play in the folklore and mythology of many countries. Or that there were so many reported cases of children who had been reared by wolves, both in India and in Europe.

What is it about the wolf that is so fascinating? Is it its strength? Its cunning? Its fierce loyalty to its young? They are feared. Powerful. Yet they are also nurturing.

A wolf walked into my dream, shortly before I started this book. It lay down beside me and watched me work. And so I kept on writing . . .

Jutta Goetze loves to observe nature. And she loves to write. She has written twelve children's books and works as a screen writer and script editor for television.

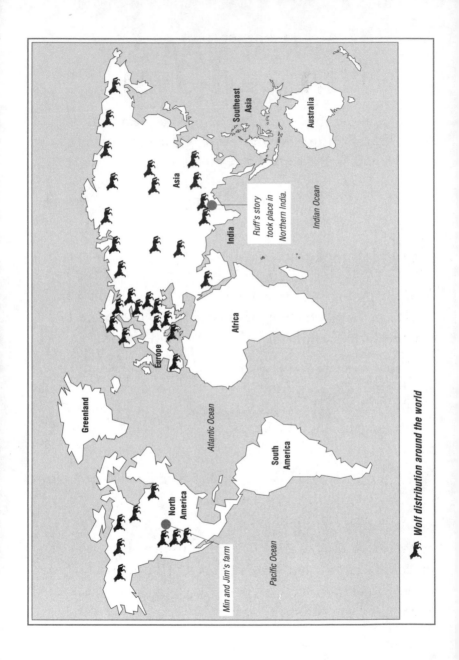

Southeast Asia

Asia

India

Ruff's story took place in Northern India.

Indian Ocean

Australia

Africa

Europe

Greenland

Atlantic Ocean

North America

South America

Min and Jim's farm

Pacific Ocean

🐺 Wolf distribution around the world

Chapter 1
Min and Jim

Fact: Pigs are very intelligent and can be taught to sit, fetch, and even play a tune on a bell.

MIN KNEW IT would be a disaster from the start.

"It's not going to work," she said. But Jim wasn't listening. He never listened to Min. He kept on bending, stretching, bending. He was taking food scraps out of a plastic bag and laying a food trail right up to the house.

"I'm a genius," he said. "It's so simple. Ellie loves food and she's greedy. All animals are." Because he was two years older than Min, he thought he knew everything.

"Why can't we just hose her down?"

"We have to conserve water. I'm using this morning's bath water." He propped open the back door. "So are you in, or what? All you have to do is keep a lookout. I'll do the rest."

"Okay." But Min wasn't convinced.

Jim showed Min where to stand, so she could warn him if anyone came. Mom was hanging out the clothes. Dad was in the barn. When Jim was ready, and the coast was clear, Min waved her hat. Jim opened the gate to Ellie's pen.

"Told you," Jim yelled as Ellie gobbled food all the way into the house. "Gotcha!" He slammed the back door shut.

Things started to go wrong when the food ran out. Ellie didn't want to stay inside. She definitely did not want to have a bath. Jim wasn't ready for a wet, complaining pig. Ellie was slippery, covered in soap, and wriggled and squirmed so much that Jim couldn't get a firm grip on her. He tried to hold her steady so he could scrub her with the pot-scrubber, but Ellie wouldn't keep still. She twisted, turned, butted Jim in the knees, and finally escaped.

By the time Min got in the house, the place was one big mess. Jim had fallen into the bath water. There was water all over the floor, now dotted with soapsud peaks. Worse, a puddle of bleach had forever changed the color of the tiles. Wet skid marks headed down the hall.

"She's in the kitchen," Jim yelled. "Oh, no, you don't!"

He rushed at Ellie, who was weaving through chairs and skidding under the table. He knocked over the cat's milk and scared the cat. Ellie's feet slipped and so did Jim's sneakers. He reached out to catch hold of her tail. Ellie flattened her ears, stretched her pink and black body, and galloped out of the way.

"Quick! She's going for the front door." Min was too late. Ellie could see the square of light and was running toward it as fast as she could. She didn't see the screen. She just kept going. The screen ripped, and the door frame banged as she charged through it.

Ellie was free. She disappeared around the corner of the house, squeezing past the gate of her pen. She stopped only when she reached the safety of the bushes. Min knew that's where she was because the branches shook for a long time while Ellie snorted her disgust.

"Where'd she go?" Jim came speeding around the corner and almost ran into Min.

"I don't know." Min felt sorry for Ellie. Jim glared at Min. He was taller than she was. And with his blonde hair shaved close to his head, he looked mean.

"Where is she, Min?" Min refused to say.

Mom and Dad arrived too late, as usual. When he saw them, Jim's expression changed. The glower disappeared. His mouth grew serious.

"What happened now?" Dad asked.

"Ellie got out," Jim said. "I found her in the house. What a mess! I had to chase her."

"The gate was closed." Min saw the frown appear between Dad's eyes. "Last time I looked."

"Min?" Mom looked at Min, who kept staring ahead. She wasn't going to tell. Min never told on Jim.

"It wasn't me."

"Min was the last one to feed her," Jim said, then.

"I wish you'd be more careful." Mom sounded annoyed. "What have we been telling you about acting responsibly? Why don't you ever listen to what we say?"

It always happened like that. Min grew angry. It was unfair. She lunged at Jim, which only made Mom and Dad yell at her and

glower: A frown or glare.

send her to her room. She stayed there, sulking and watching Jim. He was outside, playing frisbee with the dogs, Logan and Scout. He made them run after the flat pink saucer, faster, faster, until they didn't want to anymore. But he still made them run.

Min crept out of her room when she thought she'd been there long enough. She found Ellie in the shade, in a patch of earth by the barn. Ellie always went there when it was hot. She greeted Min with a snort that asked for food, sniffing her hand. Min gave her a piece of bread. She watched it disappear as Ellie swallowed it, talking in grunts all the while.

"Sorry, Ellie. It wasn't my idea. I don't think you're dirty." Min rubbed Ellie's triangle ears between her fingers, feeling the thick, rough skin, the bristles tickling. Ellie's little pig eyes seemed to be smiling. The ring in her nose, which stopped her from digging, glinted in the sun. Min sometimes thought she could understand what Ellie said.

Later that afternoon Min heard a familiar sound: the single shot of a gun, then silence. The crows flew up in a great cloud. The dogs hid under the house. They knew about guns and bullets. The animals in the pasture were restless, too. They made noises that told Min they were scared. They smelled death in the air.

Min's family slaughtered their animals for food. It could be a chicken that wasn't laying anymore or a sheep or a steer. This time it was Ellie. Dad said they wouldn't be able to eat her if she grew too old. There'd be too much fat on her. Besides, Ellie had escaped once too often. Farm animals weren't supposed to be a nuisance.

Min crept to the door of the cool room where she saw the pig's long, dark body stretched out in the shadows, hanging from a hook in the roof. Logan and Scout sat outside, whining.

"Go on—" Annoyed, Min yelled at them. "Get out of there! Get!" She gave a good kick in their direction.

She didn't go in any further, just stood, looking into the gloom. It wasn't Ellie anymore. Her eyes were blank, like stones. Min heard the drone of the flies. She saw thick, red blood drip slowly and collect in the basin below.

Min liked to eat meat. But when she saw the animals that she helped raise and that she played with dead, it made her feel sad. When she asked Dad why he had to shoot them, he told her that the nearest butcher was one hundred miles away. They had to be self-sufficient on the farm.

"Meat's nutritious," Dad had said. "Animals eat other animals to survive. That's just the way it is." It didn't seem to bother him, or Mom or Jim. No one else thought much about it, or felt the way Min did.

Min walked away from the barn and climbed into the branches of the old oak tree. She climbed as high as she could. There, right up at the top where she knew no one would see her or hear her, she started to cry. Maybe Ellie would still be alive if she'd told the truth. She was angry at herself and at Dad, and at Jim. And she was really sad. It wasn't fair. Why did Ellie have to die? So that Min could eat?

Min cried until there were no more tears. She stayed in the tree. She could see everything really clearly from up here. The peaked roofs of the house and the barns, the circles of tanks. Beside them, the ear of the satellite dish listened to the sky. Mom's few straggling flowers wilted in the garden. Beyond that, behind the fences, was the open land.

Min closed her eyes and imagined the cities that lay

> **self-sufficient**: *Capable of providing for one's own needs.*

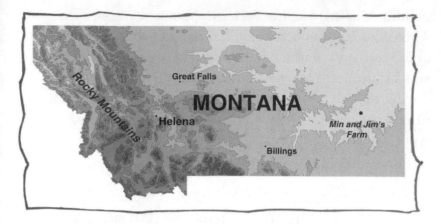

Great Falls

MONTANA

Helena

Billings

Min and Jim's Farm

Rocky Mountains

behind the horizon. She imagined the cities that were beyond the Rocky Mountains, the cities that were built right up to the edge of the sea. When she felt a breeze she thought maybe it came from there. High up in the branches, swaying, Min pretended she was a bird. A bird could fly away when it wanted to.

Min had always lived on the farm in eastern Montana. She went to school right on the farm, sitting with Jim in the study reading their schoolbooks and waiting for Mom to correct their papers. School vacations were spent helping with work. There was always too much. No matter what they did, it never seemed to get done. There weren't any neighbors nearby, at least not for a two-hour drive. There were weeks when she didn't see anyone new at all. Just Mom and Dad and Jim.

 That night Min heard heated voices that came from

behind the closed study door. Something was wrong. There was always trouble when that door was closed and Mom and Dad's voices were low. Sometimes it was because the bank wanted money. Sometimes, like during the past two summers, it was because it hadn't rained for weeks. Or it was because Mom and Dad were mad at each other. Then they would glare without talking, for days.

One time Mom was crying. A calf had died and she'd found it all bloated in a pasture, with a crow picking at its eyes. It was times like those that Mom said she'd had enough. That she was leaving.

Min heard her mother's voice.

"Jack, I don't think it's a good idea."

"He has nowhere else to go—"

"Why can't he stay in the nursing home?"

"We're family, Gwen. He wants to be with us."

Min stood at the door and listened. She learned what the problem was. Although Mom and Dad didn't want him, Grandpa was coming to stay with them.

M in was the first to see him. She had been hiding behind the oak tree, in the shade, where no one could see her. He arrived with the mailman, who brought the mail and groceries once a week from town. The dogs came charging out, barking, like they always did. Min was coming out to say hello to the mailman when she saw someone else get out. The dogs immediately ran to him, sniffing. But they didn't bark.

The man stood at the gate and looked toward the house. He was tall with stooped, rounded shoulders. He looked as if all his life he'd carried too much. As if the weight had left his back like that—humped into a curve. His arms were too long. His suit was too tight, stretching across his back. The sleeves were too short.

The old man walked slowly, carefully, like he was balancing on a tightrope and was scared he'd fall off. His hair was straggly and gray, almost white. Greasy wisps of it fell into his eyes before he pushed them back behind his ears.

"He has fur in his ears." Jim had snuck up beside Min and snorted.

Grandpa—for that is who it was—kept standing there, looking around. He turned his head from side to side. It was as though he listened with his eyes and saw with his ears. Min saw him raise his head and sniff the air. Then he bent down and patted the dogs.

"Great pair of watchdogs," Dad came out to the gate, laughing. "They usually don't welcome strangers like that."

"Dogs don't mind me," the old man said. The two dogs jumped up all over him until Dad told them to get down. Then he held out his hand.

"Hello, Dad."

"Hello, son." They hugged each other stiffly. Min studied the two men closely. Her Dad didn't look anything like the old man.

Dad walked ahead, carrying the bags. Grandpa was still looking around. Min thought he could see her because he was looking straight at her. But he didn't say anything. Maybe it was because he was looking into the sun. His eyes didn't seem to like its too-bright light. They squinted, and started to water, so that he had to wipe them.

"Dust has blown into them," he said, and was glad to go inside. The dogs dropped down onto the porch waiting for him to come back out.

"Min. Jim." Mom's voice brought them out from behind their tree. "Come and meet your grandfather. Come on."

Min waited for Jim to go. He pushed her. She had to go first. She didn't want to. There was something strange about the old man. The way he looked at things. The way he breathed aloud, like he was panting. The way his eyes didn't smile when his mouth did.

Mom said, "Russ—this is Min and this is Jim."

"Hello, Min. Hello, Jim." Grandpa formed the words slowly, carefully. Min wrinkled her nose. He smelled. It was a strange, sour smell she didn't like. He looked down at her, and his white eyebrows came together. His eyes stayed fierce.

She stretched out her hand, shy. Grandpa gripped it in his strong, cold hands. Min saw fine white lines and then jagged lines that crisscrossed the back of his hand and up his arm. They looked like old scars. His nails, really long nails, cut into her skin. She quickly pulled her hand back and stared. His nails were like claws.

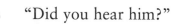

"**D**id you smell him?" Jim raced out of the house as soon as he could, ducking back behind the tree to join Min. Min screwed up her face.

"Yeah. He stinks!"

"He smells like he hasn't washed for a year! Gross."

"Did you hear him?"

"Nothin' to hear," Jim said, but Min wasn't so sure. Grandpa had talked softly, the words almost stopping inside his mouth. His voice didn't come from there. It came from somewhere else, like a growl, deep inside. But what frightened her most were Grandpa's teeth. When she was close to him she'd seen how pointy and sharp-edged the teeth were.

"I don't like him," Jim said. "I think he's weird."

Min looked back at the house. She could see Grandpa's dark shape in the window. He was standing there, looking at them.

"He's not like us," she said at last. She stayed outside until it was dark and she had to go in. Even then she didn't want to. But she didn't know why.

Chapter 2
Grandfather Russ

Fact: Farmers are more dependent on the weather than city people are. If there is no rain, crops won't grow. Animals in the wild are also dependent on the weather. If it doesn't rain, there is no grass for them to eat.

THE STRANGE NOISES began that night. As she lay in bed, Min heard the house sigh the way it always did at the end of a hot day. She heard the possum crawl out of the hole under the gutter and thump across the roof, and the dogs barking at it. A cricket that must have gotten lost and wandered into the house was still chirping loudly. From a pasture behind the barn a sheep coughed. Min knew all those sounds. It was a different sound that made her sit up in bed.

It began softly. It was close, slipping in under the other sounds. Once it started, it didn't stop. It was the quiet, almost secretive sound of footsteps walking but never getting anywhere. Footsteps going around and around, a circle that didn't end.

"Jim."

"What?"

"Listen." The steps had a steady rhythm. A shuffle, a creak when a floorboard was stood on, another shuffle. On and on. "What's that noise?"

"How would I know?" Jim was mad because Grandpa lived in his room now, and he had to share Min's. "Maybe he's a vampire."

"Don't be stupid."

"He's coming to suck your blood."

"Do you want to find out or not?" Min asked, as she quietly slid out of bed.

"Don't say I didn't warn you—"

"Shh."

"I'm not going to save you—"

"Jim! Be quiet!" She opened the door and carefully moved into the hall. A minute later Jim was beside her. Min felt her way along the wall. The house breathed loudly. In the end room, Dad was snoring. Strange sounds were coming from Jim's room.

Its door was slightly open. Min didn't know what they would find. It was as dark inside the room as it was in the hall, except for where the moonlight came through the curtains and fell softly onto the floor. And onto Grandpa, each time he walked past the window. He was taking small, shuffling steps, talking to himself in words Min couldn't understand. She pushed the door open a fraction more, so that she could see better. Her heart was thumping like a drum in her ears. Grandpa stopped, alert.

"Can't you sleep?" he said, turning so suddenly she didn't have time to duck out of sight.

"How did you know we were here?" Min asked. They'd been quiet, creeping softly in their socks. Still Grandpa knew. He'd heard them when they hadn't made a sound.

"Getting used to my new home," Grandpa said, ignoring Min's question. "Old folks like me don't need much sleep." He looked at them severely. "But you do." Min knew what Grandpa was saying—mind your own business. "Go back to bed," he said, and shooed them away.

Every night after that, Min heard Grandpa in his room. The soft wood would complain as though Grandpa was walking inside a cage.

Grandpa didn't talk much. Min and Jim grew used to that. They always had to wait for him when

22

he wanted to speak. It was as though he had
to think a lot about the words he wanted to say, and
then forgot them. Then he had to think of them
again.

"He's got a funny way of saying things," Min said
one night while they were drying the dishes after the
evening meal.

"Your grandpa spent the first twenty years of his
life in a different country," Mom replied.

"Where?"

"In India."

Min turned to look at Grandpa again. He was
hunched over the table, dipping a cookie into
his tea then eating it. He swallowed it in one gulp,
the way she had seen the dogs scoff down their food.

He was making funny
noises, too. Drops of
tea and soggy crumbs
ran out of the corner
of his mouth. He
wiped it with the back
of his hand. Min
couldn't stop staring.

"Yuk!" Jim made a
face, when he was
sure no one could see.

Min had to press her lips together really hard so she wouldn't laugh. Mom caught her and gave her a hard look, but Min couldn't help thinking "yuk!" too.

"He's old," Mom said when she and Min were alone. "And you'd better watch your manners, young lady! You be nice to him. Make him feel welcome." Mom said it in her tough voice, the one Min knew she had to listen to, or else.

Grandpa seemed to know what Min and Jim were doing all the time—even when he wasn't there. It was as though he could see around corners, or through walls.

"Why did you do that?" he asked Jim, after Jim had put the cat in the chicken coop and locked it, just to see what the chickens would do.

"I don't know. Something to do."

"Don't you think the chickens get scared?"

Jim didn't want to answer. He just shrugged his shoulders and pretended he didn't know.

Or when Min and Jim let Millie the goat into the backyard to see if she would eat the laundry off the clothesline. Millie took a nibble of a sheet, but she

24

preferred Mom's flowers. Millie got into trouble, but Grandpa knew who the real culprits were.

In the evening, when it was Jim's turn to collect eggs, he chased the chickens instead. He liked to watch them run. Min did, too. She thought the sound of their cackling was funny. She laughed when they scattered, upset, with wild looks in their eyes. Min ran and laughed because that was what Jim did. But then Jim disappeared and Grandpa came around the corner. Min was still chasing the chickens.

Min stopped immediately, flushed with running and guilt. Behind her the chickens clucked angrily, ruffled feathers flying. They scurried away with wide, scared strides. The pink skin under their beaks flapped like flags.

"Have you been scaring the hens again?"

"We're just collecting the eggs."

"They're not going to lay if you chase them like that. And they won't trust you when you come to lock them in at night," he said. Min felt ashamed. She didn't say anything. Grandpa shook his head and shuffled away.

When Jim lost his temper while feeding the calves, Grandpa was

> *culprit*: A guilty person.

suddenly there. One of the calves had kicked the feed bucket. Then the bucket hit the hoses attached to the cows being milked. The hoses fell off and milk sprayed everywhere. Jim shouted at the calf and raised his hand. He was just about to hit it when Grandpa grabbed his hand from behind.

"If I ever see you hit an animal, I'll make you sorry." His voice was shaking so much that spit flew from his mouth, and his eyes were moist and red.

"Why?" Jim's eyes were blazing, too. "They're just stupid animals." The anger in Grandpa's face died. His eyes became really sad.

"Animals are never stupid, Jim."

"Are so." Jim pulled away. "They're stupid." Then, when he got a little further away from his grandfather, he yelled, "And so are you."

After that, Jim started calling Grandpa names behind his back when he didn't think Grandpa could hear. He told Min that Grandpa was a werewolf. He said that when the moon was full, he would turn into a hairy wolf and bite Min, so she'd better watch out. Jim was scared of Grandpa and he wanted Min to be scared, too. And he did make her afraid, even though there were lots of things she wanted to ask Grandpa.

The summer wore on. It should have rained, but the rain wouldn't come. The days were blistering. The sky was a burning sheet, dusty and yellow. The water in the dam in the back pasture had shrunk to the size of a puddle. The well was running dry.

Mom and Dad worked harder and drove further to feed the sheep. Every morning they dumped hay in lines from the back of the truck. The animals stood at the fence, bleating, saying they wanted more. When there was no more, they sat in the shade of the trees, their eyes thick with flies.

One day Mom found Min in the pasture with the two dogs.

"Your dad and I are taking some sheep to the market." The tone of her voice told Min that Mom was in a hurry. Dad was already backing the truck to the pump and filling the gas tank with diesel gasoline. Min had heard them discussing the subject the night before. Dad had said they might as well shoot the sheep as sell them, for all the money they'd get.

"I'm coming, too." Min started to follow her.

"No. You're staying here with Jim and Grandpa. Make sure they get something to eat."

"I'm coming with you." Min didn't want to stay alone with Grandpa.

"Min . . ." Mom said, but Min wouldn't look.

"I want to come with you."

"Amelia Shelton, what's gotten into you!" Mom only ever used Min's full name when she was angry.

"Nothing. But I'm not staying here!" Min stubbornly stuck to her feelings. "You're not going to make me." But Mom did. Min stood there, watching the truck melt into the heat haze and disappear.

M in climbed into the oak tree. She sat up there for hours, reading and thinking. She watched Jim skulk across the yard, looking for things to do. They were both avoiding Grandpa, who was staying out of the heat, inside the house.

The sun was like a dragon curled into a red ball in the sky, breathing down fiery air. The wind had started to rise. Min rocked with the branches of her tree. A flock of crows took off from the tree by the dry creek bed. They flew toward the distant

skulk: To move around in a sneaky manner.

28

hills. After they'd gone, there was little sound. Until the back door slammed, and Min heard footsteps.

Grandpa came out of the house. He stood in the yard, turning his head until he faced into the wind. He was listening. Min could see his nostrils flare as he breathed in, smelling the messages in the stirred-up air.

He stood like that, very still, frowning. Min looked in the direction Grandpa was facing. She couldn't see anything that would make him frown. When she turned back to him, Grandpa was walking with determination. He began to round up the chickens, pushing them into their coop.

He herded the sheep next. He walked slowly over the rough stubble, calling the dogs to heel. Then he worked the dogs in a way Dad never did. They listened to his whistle and his words, nipping the sheep, pushing the herd into the pasture beside the house.

"What's he up to?" Curiosity had brought Min down out of her tree.

"Don't ask me," Jim scowled. "The sun's melted his brain."

Grandpa had trouble with the horses. The wind and the grit it was blowing up made them nervous. They shied, front hooves lifting, eye-whites showing, cantering out of his reach. But Grandpa kept walking toward them, talking softly. He didn't seem to mind the heat. And he didn't let the dogs get too near the horses.

The horses finally stopped and listened. The stallion continued to paw the ground before lowering his head and letting Grandpa catch hold of his halter. Slowly Grandpa brought them in. When he had shut the stable door, Min ran up to him. She had to know what was going on.

"Big storm's coming," Grandpa said. "We have to be ready." Min didn't believe him. There wasn't a cloud to be seen, just dirty streaks the wind had painted in the sky.

An hour later, the storm came.

Chapter 3
Ruff

Fact: Tiger hunting was a popular sport in British India until the 1920s. India won independence from Great Britain in 1945. Tiger hunting was banned in the 1950s.

MIN WENT AROUND the house twice, making sure all the doors and windows were shut tight. She stood at a window, but she could hardly see out. Streams of water were running off the panes. The sky outside had turned a dull green. Jagged cuts of forked lightning split the clouds open. Thunder growled as though it came from deep underground.

The wind that pushed at the house sounded like a train. Min saw it lift a forty-four-gallon drum and throw it down the driveway. Beyond the barn she could make out the shapes of the sheep. They were huddled in the corner of their yard, the rain pelting them. She could hear their *baas*. She was glad they were safe.

In the kitchen, the light was dim. Min flicked on a switch, but nothing happened. She picked up the phone. There was no dial tone. A tree must have fallen across the wires.

Jim came crashing in while Grandpa followed more slowly. Their hair was plastered down and their clothes were soaked. Min could smell the dogs' wet coats from under a table where they were cowering. The house was creaking. Min worried that the wind would lift it and send it flying.

"I tried to get Mom and Dad on the cell phone. I can't reach them." Jim looked frightened. "What are we going to do if they don't get back?"

"They'll be back." Min tried not to sound worried. "Why don't you and Grandpa go get into dry clothes."

After changing their clothes, Jim and Grandpa joined Min in the study.

"The electricity's out and the computer's not working," Jim replied.

"Cards?" she suggested. Jim scowled at her.

"Boring."

"Read us a story, Grandpa." Min reached for a book in the bookshelf and gave it to him.

"Just don't make it a fairy tale," Jim grumbled.

"Fairy tales have their roots in truth." Grandpa held the book carefully.

"It goes the other way," Jim said, with a smirk. Grandpa was holding the book upside down.

"Does it?" Grandpa looked at the book, turning it the other way around. "To tell you the truth," he said at last, "I can't read." He gave the book back to Min.

"Everyone can read." Min didn't believe him. Grandpa shook his head.

"Not everyone went to school in my day," he said sadly. "But I can *tell* you a story."

"I'd rather you didn't," Jim cut in. But Grandpa ignored him.

"I'd like to tell you a story. A story about a boy called Ruff."

"Why was he called Ruff?" Min asked quickly, before Jim could say anything else.

"He wasn't called that to begin with. Only later when he wouldn't listen to any other name."

"Why not?"

"He couldn't understand words. He only understood sounds. You see, Ruff was different from any boy you or anyone else is ever likely to meet. Because Ruff was raised by wolves."

"Yeah, right." Jim sat with his arms folded. "Animals can't raise kids."

"Wait until you hear the story."

"Ruff's a stupid name." Jim wanted to be difficult. "Ruff ruff. Like a dog."

"Just like a dog," the old man agreed. "Only wolves aren't dogs, even though they might look like them."

He settled into the armchair and looked at Min and Jim. His stern eyes made Jim squirm. Then he looked past them, out the window, where the sky was now black. He looked out to where the trees fought the wind, as though the story was happening out there.

"It happened a long time ago, in India, around the time I was born. And that is long ago." He spoke thoughtfully, slowly choosing his words the way he always did. But the more he talked, the more easily and smoothly the words came.

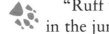 "Ruff was only two years old when he became lost in the jungle. His mother and father, who was a

doctor, had come from England to live in India. They ran a small hospital in a town in northern India. They were on a few weeks' vacation, staying with friends on a tea plantation. The owners of the plantation decided to organize a tiger hunt. Tigers still lived in the jungles of India, along with leopards and bears, hyenas, jackals, and wolves.

"A hunting party was organized. Local villagers would walk in a line ahead of the elephants, horses, mules, and bullock drays. The natives were supposed to beat their drums and blow their horns. This noise was supposed to flush out the tigers from their lairs. There weren't any cars in those days and no real roads. Just trails winding through the dry grass and tree stubble. Trails that led toward the wall of the jungle, into which no one could go.

bullock dray: *A cart pulled by a young bull.*

"It was the hot time

of year. The sun burned the sky white and baked the earth hard and dry. It was so hot that the hunting party could only travel slowly in the early morning, or in the hours just before dark. When they camped, they camped in a circle, surrounded by a ring of fires. Wild animals are afraid of fire, so the fires were to protect the people from any wild animals.

"Little Ruff traveled in a bullock dray with his mother, sitting under an umbrella to shield him from the sun. He sat like that for hours, looking out at the hills and tracts of grass and dried paddy fields. The heat had turned the rivers into twisted ribbons of brown silt and sand.

"During the day, tents would be set up in the shade, and the party would rest. They would be covered by veils of netting to protect them from the bites of mosquitoes and other insects. When the sun turned apricot and began to climb out of the sky, they would set off again. It was thought that the hunters would most likely find tigers in the evenings, before the great cats set off to hunt.

"One evening, as twilight gleamed in all of the soft colors of a pearl, the camp was packed away and the bullocks were harnessed to the

paddy field: Land on which rice is grown.

drays. Ruff woke up from his sleep and looked around. He saw a bird on the ground not far away. A reddish-brown jungle fowl was scratching at the base of a tree, making leaves and bits of grass fly up. It was looking for ants to eat. Ruff wanted a closer look.

"He climbed out of the dray he was supposed to stay in and ran along the rutted trail, his little feet pounding after the bird. But, as soon as the bird saw him it ducked out of sight in the low tangles of a lantana bush. Ruff didn't see it. He ran past it, past stands of climbing palms and bamboo. He kept going down the trail. Then he turned off onto a small path that led into the jungle.

"It was cooler and darker there. He was standing inside a great, green bell. All around him, trees reached tall into the sky. Their branches, sewn up by thick vines, spread a roof of leaves. They made a living, swaying ceiling that didn't let in any of the rays of the sun. Vines fell like swings between row upon row of tree trunks that were as thick and gray as elephants' legs. Orchids and climbing ferns grew right up into the crowns of the trees. Monkeys argued and jumped. Parrots, bright flashes of color, screeched.

"Ahead of him, Ruff could see the blue-green glimmer of a peacock. It was moving slowly between the thinner stems of young trees. Further away, a herd of small fawn-coated deer grazed at the foot of a giant banyan tree. When Ruff laughed and ran toward them, the deer raised their heads in fright. They stamped their feet, sprang into the shadows, and disappeared.

"Suddenly, Ruff heard the bullock drivers shout. He heard the voices of the villagers and the barking of their dogs. Young as he was, he knew they were moving away. He thought he heard his father's voice. He called out to him, but his father didn't hear. He started to run back, but the ground was rough. His steps were too small, and vines tripped him. Thorns hooked onto his clothes and held him. He couldn't get back. And because they didn't know he was gone, they left him behind.

"Ruff began to cry. The chainsaw drill of the cicadas started up again and drowned him out. He kept walking in the direction he thought he'd come from. But the path twisted and turned and took him further into the jungle. He cried and cried and walked and walked. No one answered him. No one came to save him.

"Long hours passed. He grew

cicada: An insect that lives in trees and makes a very loud sound.

tired and stopped walking. He stood small, still crying, hiccupping in pain and loneliness. He squeezed his eyes shut to stop the stings of the insects stuck in his tears. Everything around him was eerie and strange. He wanted to go home, but he didn't know how.

"The light began to fade. It grew darker in the jungle. A breeze stirred the tops of the trees. Leaves shivered as though they breathed. Night came, the dangerous time, when large animals woke from their sleep and started to roam.

"For the little boy, unseen monsters lurked in the dark. Plants stood nodding their heads at him, silently watching him, pointing fingers at him. A thousand hands reached out to him. Shark-tooth vines tore at his skin. He couldn't even see the ground beneath his feet. It was uneven and fell away from him. Suddenly he was standing on nothing, feeling himself fall. He landed in moss and slime and leaves. Something wriggled away from him. He stood up, started to run, and crashed down again.

"At last, when his legs hurt from running, and his throat hurt from crying, he curled up beside the silver-gray trunk of an ancient pipal tree. Tired and scared, he said one word over and over again— Mama. Mama. But his Mama didn't hear."

"**D**idn't his mom and dad look for him?" Min finally burst out.

"Of course they did," Grandpa replied. "At first they thought he was still asleep in the bullock dray. It was hours before they noticed he was gone. By the time they turned back, it was dark."

"What did they do?" Jim was interested, despite himself.

"They looked for him. But they weren't sure what had happened. Had he run off or fallen out of the dray? They didn't know where to look. And they didn't have much light, just burning rags soaked in oil attached to bamboo poles. They looked for him all night, and the next day, and the next, and the day after that. But there was no sign of their little boy."

"They must have thought he was dead," Min said, and she felt very sad.

"They did."

"Torn to pieces by wild animals," added Jim.

"That's right."

"But he wasn't, was he?"

"No. Not far away from the little boy, a she-wolf was leaving her den and the three cubs that lay asleep there. It was the first time she had hunted alone since her cubs had been born.

"The she-wolf's mate, and the aunts and uncles that make up a pack of wolves, had already left to hunt throughout the night. They had provided her food over the past weeks. Sometimes they brought back a torn piece of meat for her. Sometimes they regurgitated meat they had swallowed so that she could eat her fill. Tonight, her cubs were old enough for her to leave for a few hours so she could hunt.

"She moved quickly away from the mouth of the den, hoping nothing would see her or where she had come from. She melted into the gloom like a disappearing ghost.

"The she-wolf liked to hunt in the open grasslands, where herds of deer grazed. She preferred hunting in a pack. She relied on speed and stamina and would pick out the weakest animal in the herd and run it until it tired.

"But the summer heat had dried out the savanna. The bigger herds had moved away. The

regurgitate: To throw up or vomit.

she-wolf couldn't follow them because she had cubs to get back to at the end of the night. She had to stay close to her den. She had to make do with smaller animals—rodents, hares, and smaller species of deer—that she caught by silently stalking them.

"The she-wolf could see better in the dark than during the day. She ran easily, noiselessly along animal trails and choked jungle paths. She stopped from time to time, panting, lifting her head. Her ears would point up, so she could hear sounds that told her where animals were grazing. She moved her head from side to side so she could scent where they were. She ran into the wind so that her scent wouldn't warn the animals she was tracking and give her away.

"It wasn't long before she made her first kill. Crouching low in the thicket, she gorged herself on the flowing blood and warm flesh of a spotted deer. When there was nothing left but a patch of dark on the ground and a bit of hair and bone, the she-wolf moved on.

"Ruff had fallen into a fitful sleep. Moonlight drizzled through the leaves, making the trees silver and black. The glow turned the jungle floor into a patchwork of dark and light shadows.

"The air was thick with insects and sound. Above him, fruit bats glided silently on leather wings. A nightjar chuckled its call. The branches of the tree Ruff sat under cracked and swayed. Alert yellow eyes looked at him. A troop of gray langur monkeys with long, curving tails fed on the leaves and fruit of the pipal tree. Somewhere at the edge of the jungle came a hyena's high-pitched laugh.

"Suddenly, the sounds in the jungle around Ruff changed. From a thicket of bushes, the peacock called out its *kok kok kok* of alarm. Startled birds shot out of tree branches and flew, screeching, into the dark. The monkeys stopped chattering, nervous,

nightjar: A kind of bird.

even before their leader gave a warning cry. Danger was near. In one swift movement, the monkeys fled into the higher branches, hiding behind screens of leaves.

The ears of the jungle heard a sound, a soft footfall on leaves. The eyes of the jungle saw a shadow melt away from other shadows to become a shape. It was the shape of the she-wolf, loping slowly, carefully, toward the pipal tree. The jungle voices grew still.

"The little boy slept through the silence. The she-wolf stopped in front of him. She wasn't hungry anymore. The small, white animal in front of her didn't make her feel afraid. She could see it was young and wouldn't harm her. Lowering her head, laying her ears back, then pricking them up again, she sniffed him.

"The little boy felt the touch of her whiskers and her fur. He opened his eyes and looked into her curious amber eyes. He could smell the strong, sweet odor of blood on her breath. He didn't know he was looking at a wolf. He thought he saw a dog, an animal he knew. He was scared, but he didn't like being alone. He reached out his hand. The wolf silently bared her teeth, but she was

lope: To run with long, smooth steps.

44

also wagging her tail. She let the little boy touch her. He took hold of the fold of skin and fur under her jaws.

"'Ruff,' he said, because that's what he called his dogs at home, 'Ruff.' He stood up, swaying on unsteady, sleepy feet. He was as tall as she was, his little fingers still entwined in her fur. The wolf growled and pulled away. The movement unbalanced Ruff, who abruptly sat down in the dirt again. When he looked around, he couldn't see her anymore. He felt more alone than ever. He started to cry.

"The she-wolf heard the little boy cry. She stopped. It wasn't a threatening sound. It was a small sound that she didn't understand. It sounded like the mewings of her cubs.

"This animal she had found smelled like the human-smells she had sometimes scented, in the grasslands, on the paths. But this wasn't a dangerous smell.

"He hadn't moved suddenly when he saw her. He didn't run away, like her prey ran when it saw her. And he had looked into her eyes and didn't look away.

"The crying didn't stop. The she-wolf gave a small whine and turned around. She trotted back to the tree and sat down in front of the little boy. She watched him—ears, eyes, nose, every part of her alert. She was ready to run at any sudden movement. The little boy's tears stopped as soon as she returned. They looked at each other in silence. This time, when she moved away, Ruff stood up and followed.

"When she ran too far ahead, he cried out, and she stopped, as though she was waiting for him. When he caught up with her she sniffed him, licked his face, and went on. They moved along like this, slowly, stopping and starting. They made their way along jungle paths that ran like invisible seams through the trees.

"Sometimes they passed ant mounds that stood as high as men. Sometimes the she-wolf was hidden by the feather leaves and golden stems of bamboo. She circled around Ruff. She prodded him from behind. She pushed him on. It was as though she was herding him, making him move the same way she made her cubs move. She never left him stranded and alone.

"The entrance of the wolf's den was a large hole.

It was hidden by a mound of dirt and by the low branches of a blackthorn. The hole was inside the rotted, hollowed-out trunk of a mohua tree. In India the mohua tree is called the tree of life. The she-wolf nudged the little boy through the hole and followed him down.

"Under the earth, a large pit like a cave opened out. It was cool, dark, and clean. Tunnels led away from the center to three other entrances on different sides. Each entrance was hidden on the outside. One was hidden by the trunk of the tree, one by bushes, the last one by low, overhanging rocks.

"The den was empty, except for the she-wolf's three cubs. They were lying entwined in a soft ball of fur. When the she-wolf entered the lair, they awoke and scrambled toward her to feed. She nuzzled them, licked them clean, and lay down beside them. When Ruff lay down beside her, tired, hungry and cold, she let him.

"Seven wolves lived in the den under the mohua tree. The she-wolf and her mate, their three cubs, and two older cubs from an earlier litter. The older cubs hadn't found mates to form their own pack, so they remained with the family pack. It was a small pack because there was little food in the jungle.

"When the other wolves returned from their hunt, panting from the night's run, they were met with the unfamiliar smell of the child. They snarled at Ruff and showed their teeth. But the she-wolf lay between them and him.

"She was the leader. She talked at them with her ears back, snaking her tail. Her growls came in a warning that told them to leave the little boy alone. And they did. They curled up, in different areas of the den. Just as the sun started to rise, with a little of its light falling near the entrance, they went to sleep."

Chapter 4

Running with the Pack

"RUFF STAYED WITH THE WOLVES. For a long time he felt alone and scared. No one came for him. The jungle outside was hot and strange during the day. It was loud with the noise of cicadas and the screech of monkeys and birds. At night it was haunted by strange shapes he couldn't make out. It was alive with different sounds—the roar of a tiger, the grunt of a wild boar.

"Once he thought he heard snuffles and snorts and scratchings at the entrance of the tunnel as something tried to get in. He could dimly make out a black shape and glimmering eyes. He thought he could smell a strange, musty smell. He crawled as far back as he could, whimpering. But the she-wolf growled at him, and that made him quiet. He could see her fur bristle. She inched forward on her belly, her eyes fierce. She snarled a warning, baring her teeth.

"Whatever was outside didn't dare come in. After a while it ambled away. The she-wolf came back. As Ruff lay beside her, he could feel the beating of her heart behind her ribs and her fur. He could sense that she was scared. But Ruff knew that while she was there, he was safe in the den.

"He was hungry and thirsty all the time. Sometimes he would drink the she-wolf's milk when the cubs drank, his mouth greedy for liquid. Later, after he left the den, he learned to drink the black, cold water in the gullies from where it oozed out of the ground. During the cool season, he opened his mouth to the streaming sky. But in the beginning, he was weak. The weakness made him tired. He lay curled, with his head to his knees, against the wall of the den.

"The first time he awoke after sleeping for a long time, the den was peaceful again. The she-wolf and the cubs slept against the earthen wall. The other wolves had gone. He was hot, his face burned. But he was shivering, too. There were marks on his skin where he had been scratched by the jungle's thorns and bitten by the insects that swarmed all around.

His throat was dry. He tried to ease it by sucking his thumb. The hunger and thirst wouldn't go away.

"He moved from the wall he was crouched against. He had to find something to eat. The she-wolf lifted her head. She made a sound he didn't understand.

"He kept moving. This time the she-wolf rose from where she was lying and padded toward him. He felt her tongue wet and rough across his face. She nudged him and made a sound again. He whimpered. He still didn't understand.

"Then his hands found something soft lying beside him. He picked it up. He couldn't see in the dark, so he brought it to his mouth. He smelled it. It smelled strange. There were grains of sand on it from where it had lain on the ground. He tasted it. It was wet and slightly salty, but it didn't taste bad. It was partly chewed. He bit through the skin, and tore off a small piece. He rolled it around his mouth carefully, and slowly began to chew. Then he swallowed it and bit off another piece.

"He chewed, swallowed, bit and chewed again, until the lump of raw meat was gone. Gradually the pains in his stomach stopped, and his hunger was stilled. He curled up and went to sleep.

"From that night on, the she-wolf or one of the other wolves brought him back another piece of meat. Each had a different taste and smell. Soon he began to expect it, and he waited at the den entrance for the wolves to return.

"He began to feel stronger. He started to see better in the dark. He could make out shapes and could see when the cubs moved and where to. He knew their smell. They had grown livelier, had started to play.

They rolled around on the floor of the cave—growling, tumbling, lifting their paws, tapping. Their little jaws clamped onto and pulled little tails. Their sharp, needle teeth bit, their claws scratched.

"Ruff started to play with them. He heard his own voice and tried to make it a rolling, curling sound in answer to theirs. He didn't feel as lonely anymore.

"He was like a fourth cub. Their teeth grew sharper and scarred him when they bit him playfully. Their claws grew hard and scratched him. But he had hands, and he used them to catch hold of the cubs. He would tap them on the nose, the way they did with their paws. Because the roof of the den was low, he had to walk on his hands and knees. Ruff moved the way he saw the wolves move. Soon he forgot how to walk.

"When the cubs were old enough, the she-wolf pushed them out of the den. Ruff didn't want to leave. Unlike the cubs, he was scared. But he didn't want to stay in the den alone. When the last cub left, he followed it. He inched on his belly out into the gigantic space of night. He sat there blinking, until his eyes had grown used to the moon.

"Above him, the sky was like a tight black skin pierced by pinpricks of light. He looked for the she-wolf to tell him what he should do. He began to follow her. When she stopped to listen, he stopped and listened. When she stopped to look, he looked. When she lifted her nose to scent the air, he lifted his nose, too. Slowly the fear that had gripped him left him. Slowly he became more sure of himself.

"He liked the cool night air touching his skin. He liked to rub his back, to scratch it, against the bark of a tree. He could feel the rough ground and rotting leaves under his fingers as he walked on his hands and knees. He licked the leaves of living plants and found water on some of them. He smelled the scent of the earth. He sniffed the rich, strong smell of the fruit of the mohua tree and of the ant nest at its base.

"There were smells of other animals that had been, but were no longer, there. He found he could follow the trail of their smells. When he lifted his head to listen, he began to be aware of every sound. He noticed every movement, from the small shiver of a blade of grass, to the moving shadow of a silently swooping owl.

"Ruff learned to be ready for anything that moved suddenly or that was different or strange. That could mean danger, and in danger, he knew he had to run.

"Soon, Ruff and the cubs left the den every night. As they grew stronger and braver in their knowledge, they began to follow the paths of the jungle and the highways of scent. Sometimes these led to an animal, which they chased, running when the she-wolf ran.

54

That is how they learned to hunt.

"Muscles developed in Ruff's legs and arms. He grew sinewy. The clothes he wore no longer fit him. They ripped and fell off. When he wanted to move quickly, he learned to come off his hands and knees to run on his hands and feet.

"He wasn't as fast as the adult wolves, so he had to stay near the den. But he was no longer scared to explore or patrol. Then, when the first bright rays of the sun pried open the sky, he returned to the den. There he curled into a ball alongside the cubs, and slept.

"The longer Ruff stayed with the wolves, the more he began to sound like them. He learned to understand the wolf-language of whines and snarls and snaps and growls that told him what he could and could not do. He learned the silent language of bared teeth and of the movement of their tails. He knew what their howls meant when the howls came from far away. He learned how to howl, too.

"Because he ate the same food the wolves did, because he lived with them, he began to smell like them. But he never looked like them. His skin became browner, dirtier. Pads of tough, leathery skin grew on his knees and

> **sinewy**: Muscular; strong.

hands. His hair grew long and tangled, but he never had any fur. And he didn't grow as fast or run as far as the other three cubs.

"In two years, when the others had become adults, they moved away from the pack. But Ruff didn't leave. Instead, he stayed to play with and look after the next litter of cubs the she-wolf had. He remained to drink her milk again, to curl asleep with the cubs, to eat the meat that she and the other wolves brought them.

"There were other things he learned watching them. He kept clean by licking his hands and rubbing his skin. He knew where the water holes covered in reeds and water lilies were, where animals came to drink. He knew to look out for crocodiles, to crouch low near the water and wait.

"He knew that to eat, he had to hunt. He learned to stalk an animal. He learned to wait for the right moment, when the animal was unaware, so that he had the element of surprise. He knew how to run at it and startle it, how to work with the other wolves to corner it. He knew how to kill it by ripping it with his teeth. He knew that to eat his fill, he had to eat quickly, before the other wolves could chase him away.

 "He ate rocks and pebbles, the way the wolves did. He ran snarling at the vultures who always came gliding by and hopping around when there had been a kill. He learned to hide a kill too big to eat all at once. He'd pull it into a thicket and scratch bark, dirt, and leaves over it. Sometimes, when he had traveled too far to return to the den, he would find a dark place to curl up in. He slept long after every kill.

"Ruff knew the signs that told him when the rains would come, when he had to move to higher, drier ground. He knew how to heal a wound by licking it. He knew how to find a safe, dark place and stay there when he did not feel like running, or when he was ill. He scratched at ticks and fleas, catching them with his nails and teeth.

"He learned the signs of danger. He knew to avoid the cobra and the living strings. These were the deadly emerald-green tree snakes that hid in the branches and leaves of the jungle trees. He knew the danger of the tiger. He understood what the wolf pack's growls meant when they smelled the scent of another wolf that didn't belong to their pack, hunting in the territory that was theirs.

"Ruff knew his place in the pack that had become his family. Gradually, he began to forget he was a boy."

Grandpa's voice fell silent. Min waited for more, but there was only silence. She looked up. It was dark outside. The wind didn't sound as fierce, and the house wasn't shaking as much. Lightning still flashed occasionally. The thunder still growled. Min flicked a light switch, not hoping for much. Nothing happened.

"Looks like we need some light," Grandpa said. Min realized he wasn't asleep.

Jim found an old kerosene lamp, some fuel, and matches. Soon, light and warmth filled the room. The dogs crawled out from under the table and sat at Grandpa's feet. He was rubbing their ears. Min couldn't stop looking at Grandpa's hands.

"Grandpa," she said, her voice shaking a little, "Where did you get those scars?"

Grandpa looked at his hands. The white lines stood out, crisscrossing the folds of his old skin.

"They're just scars," he said. "I got them from a lifetime's hard work."

"Did anything ever bite you?" Min pushed.

"Yes, I was bitten—" Grandpa started to say.

"By a wolf," Jim jumped in. "I knew it!"

 Grandpa didn't reply. He was talking to the dogs.

Chapter 5

Caught

> *Fact*: Wolf packs have a well-structured family system. Only the lead females have cubs. Wolves form emotional attachments to their young, and they are fiercely loyal and protective.

MIN FOLLOWED JIM into the kitchen. He had his back to her. He was sawing at something with Mom's best kitchen knife. As she came closer, Min saw he was cutting up a piece of raw meat.

"What are you doing?"

"I want to see what happens." Jim carried the plate with the meat on it back into the study. He put it on the small table, not too far away from Grandpa.

"Did Ruff ever get caught?" Min sat down.

"Oh, yes." It took a while for Grandpa to reply. "Otherwise, how would anyone have found out about him?"

"How'd he get caught?" Jim couldn't help himself.

He had to know.

"Well," Grandpa saw the meat Jim had left on the table. He picked the pieces up, and held them as though it was his fingers, not his eyes, that were looking. Then he gave each of the dogs a piece.

"W hen Ruff saw human beings again, he had been living with the wolves for four years. It was a hungry time in India. The rains were late, the way they were here. There wasn't much grass around. The herds of animals the wolves hunted had moved away.

"Now the wolves had to travel further and further to find food. This brought them closer to villages and to village fields. Sometimes they killed a goat that hadn't been safely put behind the bamboo and stick fences at night. Ruff smelled the human-smell for the first time in years, in the riverbeds and on the village paths. In the distance, at night, he saw lights that did not come from the sky. They seemed to move and dance on the ground. He smelled the smoke of fires.

"As soon as the wolves scented the human-smell, they grew wary. They began to pace nervously in circles, ears flat, tails down, fur quivering, making small, frightened sounds. For Ruff, it was a lesson in fear. The wolves, frightened only of the crocodile, the tiger, and the bear, did not like to come near the human-smells. But, as the heat wore on, hunger overcame fear, and they moved closer still.

"The first time Ruff saw the two-legged animals, they were far away. They were riding other, faster, four-legged animals, carrying sticks that flashed with fire. He soon associated with men the short, sharp sound that silenced the jungle and hurt his ears.

"There were other animals with them. Smaller animals with fur and four legs and tails, heads with ears and lolling tongues. They ran behind the men. They barked and yapped and yowled, ran like wolves and looked like wolves, but didn't smell like wolves. When these animals sensed the wolves, they ran to attack them with hate in their eyes.

"Ruff was by himself the next time he saw men. He was on a track at the edge of the jungle, where it was easier to run. The Great Dry had forced the villagers to look for roots and fruits and berries further away from their village. Their search took them to a part of the jungle where they would not normally go.

"It was getting dark when they saw a creature ahead of them, sitting on its haunches, all elbows and knees. Its head was huge in a mass of hair. Two terrible eyes stared at them. When they saw him, they ran. Ruff, when he saw them, ran too.

"After that villagers didn't walk by themselves anymore. They tied empty kerosene cans to the bottom of their bullock drays to make a lot of noise. The sound of the cans bumping over the ground was supposed to scare the ghost away. That's what they thought Ruff was: a ghost.

"They believed in ghosts. They thought the forest was haunted. They began to blame Ruff for the late rains. They said that he was cursed. They made sure they always carried their kudi with them, as a weapon and not as a spade.

"News spread of the creature in the forest. Others saw that it ran with the wolves. They followed it to the den under the mohua tree. They knew where it lived.

"The villagers wanted the ghost to go away. But they didn't want the wolves killed. They believed that spilling a wolf's blood anywhere near their village would stop their crops from growing. So they decided to catch the ghost. They asked men from other villages to come with them. Some of them were hunters. One of them had a gun.

"The wolves heard the villagers coming and heard their dogs. The

kudi: A tool used by Indian villagers for digging and hoeing.

wolves crowded into the den against the wall that was furthest away from the sounds. Their hearts beat loudly, their eyes showed their fear. Ruff cowered with them, crouching against the earth, hidden by their bodies.

"It grew dark. The wolves could smell the smoke of the oil and rag flares the villagers carried. Still they didn't move. Only the she-wolf prowled around the den, moving from entrance to entrance. She drew back her lips, letting out a low growl. Suddenly, the wolves heard the strike of a spade in soil. The villagers had started digging into the earth of the den.

"The wolves moved then. The lead male ran to the farthest entrance. He could hear the villagers on the other side, away from this opening. He crawled through and broke free. He hadn't been seen. Hidden by the thicket of the forest, he let out a short yelp.

"Inside the den, the other wolves pricked their ears. The second wolf followed. Then the younger wolves broke out of the earth and disappeared into the smoke-filled night.

"A cry of voices rose. The villagers had seen the last wolf go. Only the she-wolf and Ruff remained in the den. The she-wolf growled continuously, a low sound filled with panic and fear. She ran from one entrance to the next. But the men had moved around now and surrounded the den.

"With an angry bark she sprang out of the den. She stayed in a low position as she ran at the dogs and the spades. She bared her teeth, snapped at legs, and snarled viciously before returning to the safety of the den. Ruff hadn't moved. The she-wolf nudged him urgently. Again she rushed out, her tail whipping, her bristles standing, the rows of her teeth exposed. This time Ruff followed her, snarling like she did, growling the same warnings, showing his teeth.

"Another shout rose. The men began to close in, their spades and weapons raised. Sensing a break in the line, the she-wolf ran for that. But Ruff was too frightened to move.

"When she realized he wasn't coming, the she-wolf

spun around. When she saw the men turning toward him, she launched herself to attack. The man who carried the gun had no choice but to raise it, fire it. The she-wolf's body fell to the ground.

"Ruff forgot about the villagers. He ran to where she lay. He watched as the she-wolf, his mother, closed her eyes. He watched her breath stop and the blood leave her body and seep into the dusty ground. Her body was still there, but she wasn't. He felt pain. It wasn't a physical pain. It came from his head and his heart. It ripped through his chest. He did not understand. He felt water leak from his eyes. He didn't know what it was."

"She was dead." said Min.

"I know that." Jim said impatiently.

"But Ruff didn't have any words to understand that. He didn't even have thoughts, the way we do. All he knew was that it was the fire in the men's sticks and the big sound the fire made—the sound which the wolf pack had been the most afraid of—that had taken the she-wolf away.

"The other wolves were gone. Ruff stood alone, facing the circle of villagers. He hissed at them and snarled, gnashing his teeth, pulling the most ferocious faces they had ever seen. When they came too close, he clawed at them. When they tried to catch hold of his hands, he swiped at them and bit them when he could.

"They could only catch him by throwing a net over him, dragging him down, and pinning him. With difficulty they tied his hands and feet, carried him to a bullock cart, and heaved him in. They left the net around him and weighted it down with a stone. Only then did they inspect the thing they had caught. When the creature looked at them, they knew it wasn't a ghost they were seeing. They saw a wolf looking out through the eyes of a boy.

"Slowly, the villagers made their way back home. They followed the rough, bumping tracks through the high grass jungle and dusted rice paddy fields. The sun had risen halfway into the sky by the time they reached their village. It was small, set behind the safety of a thornbush and bamboo stockade. Identical huts were made of mud and dung and had high, thatched roofs. A clump of feathery-leafed tamarind trees gave the village its shade.

"Women and children gathered around the bullock cart to see what the hunters had caught. Ruff lay on his side, his eyes shut. He didn't know what was happening to him. He was paralyzed with fear. He didn't like the smells of the village. Its sounds were strange to him. He felt his heart hammering inside his chest. He whimpered as the villagers poked him with sticks and the butts of their spears, pushing him out of the dray.

"The hut he was put into was in the center of the village. There was one large room, a space much bigger and higher than the space in the wolves' den. Flies hung in clouds around the windows and the door, which let in too much light. The sun hurt Ruff's eyes. It made water leak from his eyes. He pinched his eyes closed and tried to turn his face away.

"He wanted to run outside where the trees grew, along the paths he knew.

bamboo stockade: *A strong fence made of bamboo posts pushed upright into the ground.*

He wanted to sleep in the den where he had been safe. He missed his family, the wolves. He looked for them, sniffing the ground, searching the corners of the room. When he couldn't find them, he moved to the darkest part of the room and tried to hide. He stayed like that, sitting facing the wall, silent and alone.

"That night, and every night for weeks after he had been caught, the wolves circled the village and howled. And every night, the wolf-boy howled back. It was a sound that began low in his throat. Then it rose into a long, drawn-out cry filled with sorrow and despair. Soon the monsoon rains began. But nothing changed for Ruff.

"He didn't eat. He wouldn't let anyone near. He spat out the green coconut water they pushed into the hut. He didn't want any of their sweet milky tea. He would only lap water left in an open pan. He would come at it on his hands and knees, sniff it, and drink it in great thirsty gulps until there was nothing left.

> **monsoon**: Intense seasonal rains, which in India come in their summer—December to February.

"For many weeks he sat facing the corners of the hut, moving when the sun grew too bright. He grew weaker and thinner. Yet he still turned away from the bowls of rice and vegetables and chapattis, the flat, pancake-shaped bread that was left for him. He didn't like the smell of spices. He didn't know that it was food.

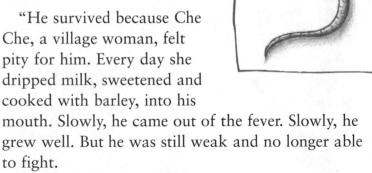

"He became very ill. He was in a fever that the villagers thought was rabies because he had been living with the wolves. But he didn't die.

"He survived because Che Che, a village woman, felt pity for him. Every day she dripped milk, sweetened and cooked with barley, into his mouth. Slowly, he came out of the fever. Slowly, he grew well. But he was still weak and no longer able to fight.

"One day when she came to feed him, Che Che saw the wolf-boy crawl toward a lizard lying in the hut in a patch of sun. He watched it, staying at the edges of the shade, moving forward slowly, carefully. He pounced, pushed the lizard against the wall, and caught hold of it in his mouth. He ate it.

"Che Che realized that what Ruff wanted was raw meat. He had been slowly starving because she hadn't known what to give him to eat. From then on, he ate what the village dogs ate. He ripped at chunks of meat, gulping them down. Then he would take the bones into the corner of the room to chew and gnaw and paw at them.

"Che Che gave Ruff his name. He had been sitting watching Pachu, a little boy, playing with the dogs. Ruff looked up, alert, each time Pachu called to one of the puppies: 'Ruff. Ruff.' It was as though the wolf-boy knew that sound.

"'Ruff, Ruff,' Che Che said to him. He looked at her then quickly looked away. 'Ruff'—she said it again and he looked again. From then on, she called him Ruff and he gradually learned to respond.

"Che Che sat with Ruff and talked at him. She tried to stroke him, but he bared his teeth at her and didn't let her near. She tried to bathe him because he smelled and was covered with lice and fleas. Ruff didn't like water touching him. He struggled and fought while Che Che poured water over him. Eventually, she cleaned away the dirt that was like a hard crust on his skin. She found that he was covered in scars.

"She managed to trim his nails, which had curled around and were long and strong like claws. She cut the tangle of hair and thorns and dirt that was like a nest around his head. With his head shaved almost clean, Ruff looked more like a child than the monster the villagers had thought he was.

"Ruff wouldn't sleep in a bed. He would lay curled up on the floor. He scratched at the clothes he was made to wear and tore them with his teeth. He grew restless every night when the hurtful sun was gone. When the moon streamed in through the window, his eyes could see.

"He walked on his hands and knees, around and around, prowling endless circles. He could see images of the wolves in his head.

prowl: To roam as if looking for something.

He could see them even though they had gone. He did not understand why.

"As the weeks passed, he started to notice the things going on around him. He learned to make a sound that told Che Che he was hungry. He licked his lips when there was no water in the room, which told her he wanted to drink. He waited for her at the door of the hut when it was time for him to get his food. But he still smelled his food first, before bolting it down.

"Ruff learned quickly that the door was where Che Che came in and out. The door was what he had to get through in order to return to the jungle, and to the wolves. He began to listen for sounds outside it, began to watch for its movement when it opened and to rush at it as soon as it did. But Che Che seemed to know that that's what he would do, and she was always ready for him.

"When the days grew too warm, he was placed in an enclosure outside, a cage made of poles, branches, bamboo, and thorns. It was too high for him to jump over.

"The village children threw stones at him and poked sticks at him. He was too different, too strange. He had white skin. He didn't talk like them. He didn't walk like them. He smelled and made strange noises. He ran at them, making faces if they came too close. The children laughed at him, called him names, and chased him. But they never came too close. They were afraid of Ruff.

"People said that when a light shone in the dark, his eyes glowed. Not from the reflection, but a glow that came from inside."

"Like a fox's eyes!" Min remembered the red eyes that shone bright at night when their car passed a fox on the side of the road.

"Dog and cat eyes shine, too." Jim wouldn't let her beat him with what she knew.

"Yes," Grandpa said. "Animal eyes, when you shine a light at them, reflect the light. People's eyes don't."

Min looked carefully at Grandpa's eyes to see if they glowed, too. But Grandpa caught her looking and she quickly looked away.

"I don't know," Grandpa added, "if that part of the story is true. Sometimes, people's imaginations get carried away." When he said that, he seemed to stare especially hard at Min and Jim.

"For hours on end, Ruff would only sit and stare straight ahead. He didn't smile because he didn't feel joy. He didn't scowl because he didn't feel anger. The only time his expression changed was when he was scared. The only time he looked like he was maybe enjoying himself was in the evenings when he was alone in the village yard, before he was locked inside his hut. With no one around, he thought he was free. Then he would raise his head and cry his lonely cry to the moon.

"Ruff slowly made friends with the village dogs. He never made friends with people. He remained frightened and wary of the beings that walked on two legs. Their voices sounded harsh and strange. They made sounds he couldn't understand. They wouldn't let him out of the cage.

"But Ruff's life changed when the elephants came."

Chapter 6

Coming Back from the Wild

Fact: Indian elephants have smaller ears and smaller bodies than African elephants. Elephant herds consist of females and their young. Bulls usually live alone.

"Have you ever seen an elephant's footprint? It's like a map of the world."

"How do you know?" Jim responded.

"I've seen one in the sand. I've tracked an elephant across the land. An elephant's footprint is like your fingerprint, just as individual as you are. You know how big an elephant is by the size of its prints." Grandpa circled his arms out in front of him to show how big an elephant's footprint could be.

"It has lines on it, like the lines of a map, with roads, craters, rivers, and hills. But the patterns are fine, as fine as the veins in a leaf." Grandpa's eyes lit up in a way Min hadn't seen before. There was wonder in them. And a smile.

Min had never seen an elephant. She'd never even been to a zoo. She closed her eyes and tried to imagine . . . its skin, thick and gray and rough, like the bark of a tree. Tusks of yellow ivory like long, thin half-moons, that could reach down, almost to the ground. Big ears like flags, eyes like pig eyes, small for such a big head. Elephants smiled with their eyes, Grandpa said. They were wise.

"**B**ut sometimes elephants get sick, or they're injured, or they're in pain. Sometimes, in a drought, the rivers become sand, and there's nothing to eat for the herds of deer or the goats or even the cows. When the elephants have torn down all the trees and ripped up all the stringy grass, when there's nothing left for something so big to eat—sometimes that can make an elephant crazy.

"No one really is sure what happened that night. If you went to India now to find someone who was there, you probably wouldn't find anyone because it

drought: A long period with no rain.

happened so long ago. But rumor has it that the wolf-boy called the wolves together. That he and the wolf pack saved the village from the elephants.

"How do you know, if no one else does?" Jim's eyes were narrow with suspicion. "Were you there?"

"I was in India," the old man replied.

"The villagers' millet and rice was almost ready to harvest. Night and day villagers perched on wooden platforms called watchtowers, guarding the crops against animals and birds.

"But it was Ruff, with his keen sense of hearing, who heard the elephants first, even though they were still far away. He began to restlessly run along the fence of his cage. He began to growl. And then to howl. From the jungle came the howls of wolves in reply.

"The cry from the fields, the shouted voices, came soon after. These were followed by the crack of wood, like matchsticks.

millet: A type of grain.

Then the trumpeting call that no one could mistake. The villagers, who had been asleep in their huts, ran into the fields to save their crops. Only the old women and children too young to help, and Ruff, locked in the cage, were left behind.

"Ruff continued to howl. He had heard the wolves again. They were near and he wanted to be with them. He ran backward and forward, pawing at the earth. He tried to find a small hole in the fence to poke his head through, to push his shoulders through. He began biting the wood, rattling it, turning from it to run and jump at it. Finally, after constantly crashing the full weight of his body against it, the wood splintered, and he was free.

"In a burst of speed, he ran the way he used to run in the jungle, on hands and feet. He sprinted through the village gate and onto the dusty path outside the wall. He heard the voices of the villagers, heard their cries as the elephants stampeded through their fields. He heard the elephants' rolling growls. They were close. But the jungle was close, too. All he had to do was turn in that direction and run, and he would be free.

stampede: *A sudden rush of panic-stricken animals.*

"The elephants' footfalls thudded dully on the trail. Giant, gray beasts

plunged out of the dusky night. They were larger
than anything he had ever seen. He heard their
breaths, like engines, and their call, deep and
guttural. He heard branches and trees crack and
break as the elephants were charging. Ruff started to
howl once more.

"Suddenly, five dark shapes appeared, running at
the leader of the elephants. Ruff sprang out of the
way. And then ran with the shapes, sinking teeth
into tough hide. The huge elephant raised its trunk
and blasted an angry sound at them, rolling its head
from side to side. But, it faltered and, at the last
minute, swerved.

"The wolves continued to chase it. The rest of the
elephant herd followed its leader. Instead of coming

into the village, they ran along the side fence, down the trail, and disappeared into the choppy grass sea. The women and the children in the village were saved.

"It was the last time the wolf-boy ever saw the wolves. They disappeared as silently as they had come. He remembered the familiar panting of one thin, tall wolf that remained behind. Remembered the way it had loped toward him, after the elephants had gone. It was a brother. They had played together when they were young, rolling on the earthen floor of the den under the mohua tree. And later, they had run together in full flight through the jungle, stalking deer.

"The wolf now eyed him warily. It skirted him, sniffing him. Ruff made sounds to it, which the wolf seemed to half understand. It drew nearer, its nose touched Ruff's skin. But when Ruff moved, it leaped back. The villagers began returning. They thudded through the undergrowth, talking loudly in excited, frightened voices. The wolf backed into the forest and was gone. It never returned. No matter how loudly Ruff howled, he was never answered.

"The villagers treated Ruff differently after that night. He had saved them and he was to be honored. Ruff was now accepted, strange as he was.

"Months passed. A year. The monsoon rains came again, making the brown land green. The rivers swelled like great writhing snakes and brought tides of silt down from the mountains. The silt remained behind when the water dried up, and the villagers planted their crops in the ooze of soft mud and slime. The sun grew hot again. The rice grew, was harvested, and dried on patches of earth, amongst great stacks of hay.

"Ruff's fear of the villagers dimmed with the passing of time. Their smell did not repulse him anymore. They did not harm him. They continued to feed him. They made noises at him that he began to understand. Slowly, he grew used to a different rhythm of life.

"Every morning he watched the children run to the village tank to wash. Village women walked slowly behind them, carrying earthen jars on their heads, talking, laughing, calling out to the children.

"Ruff could pick out the woman, Che Che, who fed and talked to him and was kind to

silt: Rich soil.

him. He saw the shepherds lead their goats through the enclosures beside the village compound and along paths, to the grasslands further away. He saw dust rise and mix with the smoke of the cook fires.

"Every night, when the sun dimmed and the light turned purple, the shepherds returned with the goats, and the dust swirled again. Children played beside his cage. Some of them even came in to sit with him. From far away came the tinkle of a temple bell. Ruff had lost his fear of the sun and woke with it, falling asleep with the rising of the moon.

"His fame spread. More and more people heard about the strange wild boy who had come out of the jungle. Sadhus, holy men who walked from village to village begging for food, spoke his name.

"The troops of jugglers and singers and acrobats who traveled on India's roads told his story. Missionaries heard about him. Traders and cowherds brought news of him to the markets and village fairs. People came from great distances just to look at the boy in the cage."

"Did his parents ever find out about him? His real parents?"

82

For a moment it didn't seem that Grandpa had heard what Min asked. His eyes were looking into a place that was far away. Then he nodded.

"Yes, they did. His parents found him again after having lost him for five years."

"Did they recognize him?"

"No, I don't think so. The changes were so great. Although a mother will tell you that she will always know her son."

"What did they do?"

"When they came to the village, he was squatting in the dirt by the gate. When they saw him, both of them cried. They thanked God in heaven for finding him again. They took him back to the hospital where they could take care of him."

"Did he learn to become a person again?" It was Jim who asked. A smile flickered across Grandpa's face.

"**D**octors and scientists came from England and America to examine Ruff and to write papers about him, which they then published in journals. Wherever he was, people stared at him, whispered about him.

"But it wasn't doctors or scientists or speech therapists who taught Ruff what he needed to learn. It was patience, determination, and love. Ruff had to unlearn his animal ways before he could become human again. His parents loved him. They wanted him to have what everyone has a right to have—a good life. And so they taught him everything. They taught him how to walk, how to talk, how to feel. They began at the beginning, as though he were a baby."

Grandpa looked at Min and at Jim.

"**W**hat do you think it's like not to be able to read a book or a poem? To not know how to dance to music, or how to draw, or to sing a song? What if you couldn't speak to say what you feel? Imagine not knowing what it's like to feel. To not know what's funny or sad. What if the only things you knew were taught to you by wolves? If nobody else could understand the sounds you made? Only the wolves Ruff had lived with could understand Ruff's sounds. And the wolves were no longer there."

Min shut her eyes. She tried to imagine it, but she couldn't.

"And how to trust, how to love, how to think—how do you learn those?"

Min shook her head. She didn't know.

"It took a long, long time. There were many disappointments. They had to do many things again and again. There were many things Ruff could never learn. But gradually he grew to depend on his parents the way he had depended on the wolves. He learned to smile when he saw them come into a room. To nod for yes, to shake his head for no, and to understand what those gestures meant. He began to reach for food with his hands and to talk with his hands because he still had no words.

gesture: A bodily motion or sign.

He began to know what things were and to touch them when he wanted to show his parents what he meant.

His knees straightened with exercise and the unused muscles grew. He learned to stand, weaving like a tree in a strong wind because at first those muscles in his legs were so weak. He took his first steps holding onto his parents' hands. Then he learned to walk without holding on. Finally, he learned to talk, but some of his words would always be slow.

"The years rolled on. A war began and ended. In time England no longer ruled India, and the English went home. Ruff and his parents traveled to the much colder country of England on a great ship. There were so many new things to learn there, new tastes to taste, new sounds to hear. New things to see. For the first time in his life he saw the white rain fall. When he reached out and caught hold of it, he laughed because it melted away in his hands.

"The time with the wolves started to fade. He forgot about them for hours, then days. As he learned more and more about the ways of people, he began not to think about the wolves at all. But when he least expected it, a smell or a sound would suddenly spring at him and remind him. Sometimes it was the way a dog ran ahead of him in the street. Even the silent movement of the moon through the trees brought the pictures of the wolves back into his head, and water would leak from his eyes.

"He remembered all too clearly the way the moonlight had fallen onto the earth and onto the forest floor. He remembered how it had glowed in the flecks of the she-wolf's eyes. He remembered those eyes, near to him for so many years. He remembered everything and missed everything. The roughness of the she-wolf's tongue over his skin. The touch of her fur. The smell of her. The taste of her milk. The sound of her growls, the language of her movements and sounds.

"He felt the pain again, nearly as strong as the pain he felt when the she-wolf died. Somewhere in the fog of his mind, where thoughts were beginning to form more clearly, he knew that he would never see that life again."

The old man was quiet. This pause was much longer than the pauses for breath that had stopped the story before. The circle of light the kerosene lamp threw onto the table was getting smaller and weaker. The storm had passed. The rain had thinned. But the gutters still overflowed where Dad hadn't pulled out the leaves and grass. Every now and then, the oak tree shuddered, and a load of water thundered onto the roof.

Min stretched. It seemed as if days, months, even years had passed, as though she had been away for a very long time.

"And?" said Jim. He had not taken his eyes off the old man. "What happened then?"

"What do you think happened?"

"It's your story," said Jim.

"The world forgot about Ruff."

"But—" Min's eyes were big and round with the pictures in her head.

"No buts. That's how some stories end." Grandpa looked at them, stern. "Or would you have preferred it if people constantly stared at him, prodded him with their questions, never leaving him alone?"

"No," Min said in a small voice.

"For many years Ruff was lost to the world of humans. He'd been brought out of the wild back to a place where he didn't belong. He had lost precious years, the years in which children learn to speak, to think, to do, to be. Ruff didn't learn the answer to

 88

the words that asked—Who am I? So that's what he set out to do. He spent the rest of his life trying to find out."

"Did he find out?" Min asked softly.

"I hope so," the old man said.

At that moment, the radio blared on in the kitchen. The refrigerator coughed and began to hum. "I guess the power's back on," Grandpa said. Not long after, they could see truck headlights dip and bounce over the bumps in the drive. Mom and Dad were home.

Min and Jim didn't go to sleep right away. There were still too many noises in the house. There were Mom and Dad's voices in the room at the end of the hall, as they talked before they went to sleep. There was the rattle of the wind as it shook some loose shingles. There were the sounds of the possum crawling back under the roof. And then there was that other sound that Min had come to know. It was the sound of footsteps on the floorboards, steps that wouldn't stop, pacing round and round.

"Is it true?" Min asked softly.

"It's just a story," said Jim.

"Some stories are true."

"Not this one." But Jim's voice didn't sound so sure.

Min lay in bed, thinking. Outside, the clouds ripped apart and the moon that was hiding behind them appeared. Min slipped out of bed. She crept into the hall and walked noiselessly down it, toward Grandpa's room. Like she'd done once before. The door was ajar. She pushed it a little more, so that she could see inside.

Grandpa wasn't asleep. He was pacing around the room, as Min knew he would be. The light from the moon caught his face each time he passed the window. It made his eyes bright. When he stopped walking and stayed at the window, he cocked his head to hear the sounds from outside. Then he made sounds from deep in his chest. Min saw tears in his eyes.

That was when Min knew. It was a picture in her head that she couldn't explain. She only knew that it was true. She walked into the room and put her arm around the old man. She made him put his arm around her. She snuggled into his armpit, into his side.

"It's all right, Grandpa." Her voice was small. "I'm here."

And then Jim came, too.

Animal Facts

Animals such as cats, wolves, and foxes have a reflective layer inside the eye that shines if it is caught by a light. This layer makes the best of poor light so the animals can see in near darkness.

A peacock, known for its colorful tail that it can raise and spread, is a native of India. Peacocks are now often kept as tame display birds. The male is called the peacock and the female is called the peahen.

Wolves are fully grown at two years of age and leave the pack to find a mate. If the mate dies, or if they are unable to find a mate, they stay with the pack as "uncles" and "aunts." Wolves live up to ten years.

There are only about one thousand wolves in India today. The number of them in many parts of the country is reduced because their habitat has been destroyed and there is less wild prey for them to eat.

The lead or dominant female wolf in the pack is called the alpha female. Her partner, the lead male wolf, is called the alpha male. The lowest ranking wolf is called the omega wolf.

Wolf packs hunt in their own territory, which can be up to fifty square miles in size. They mark their territory with urine and droppings. Like wolves in the wild, domestic dogs also mark out their territory with scent secreted from glands at the base of their tail.

Wolves use sounds—whimpers, squeaks, barks, and growls—to call their pups together, to calm them, and to warn them of danger. The howl calls the pack together.

Indian elephants live only in southern and southeastern Asia. An adult Indian bull stands from 9 to 10 1/2 feet tall at the shoulder and weighs up to 8,000 pounds.

Indian elephant

African elephant

Wild African elephants live only in Africa, south of the Sahara. An adult African bull stands about 11 feet tall at the shoulder and weighs about 12,000 pounds.

Where to from Here?

You've just read the story of one boy's amazing experiences with animals.
Here are some ideas for finding out more about human-animal relationships.

The Library

Some books you might enjoy include:
- *The Black Stallion*, by Walter Farley
- *Sounder*, by William Armstrong
- *Balto and the Great Race*, by Elizabeth Kimmel
- *Julie of the Wolves*, by Jean Craighead George

Here's a nonfiction book to try:
- *Dolphin Adventure*, by Wayne Grover

TV, Film, and Video

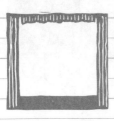

Check TV listings and ask at a video store or your library for films in which people interact with animals. A few suggestions are:
- *Babe*
- *Homeward Bound: The Incredible Journey*
- *Free Willy*

The Internet

There is a wealth of information on the Internet. Here are some key words you may want to start with: *animals, animal myths, fables.*

People and Places

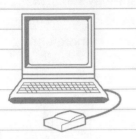

Ask family and friends for their stories about animals. Zoos and science museums are other sources of great animal information.

The Ultimate Nonfiction Book

Be sure to check out *Animal Attack,* the companion volume to *Wolf Cry. Animal Attack* tells you some facts you'll never forget about the ways that people and animals relate to each other.

Decide for yourself
where fiction stops
and fact begins.